OPERATION
RAWHIDE

CREATION ADVENTURE SERIES

OPERATION RAWHIDE

The Dramatic Emergency Surgery on President Reagan

PAUL THOMSEN

INSTITUTE FOR CREATION RESEARCH

SANTEE, CALIFORNIA

Unless otherwise noted, all Scripture quotations are from the New King James Version of the Bible, © 1979, 1980, 1982, 1984 by Thomas Nelson, Inc., Nashville, Tennessee, and are used by permission.

Illustrations by Brian Thompson

Institute for Creation Research
P.O. Box 2667
El Cajon, California 92021
1 (800) 628-7640

Library of Congress Cataloging in Publication Data

Thomsen, Paul M., 1938—
    Operation rawhide / Paul Thomsen—2nd ed.
    p. cm.— (Creation adventure series)

    Summary: A fictionalized account of President Reagan's assassination attempt in 1981, focusing on the life-saving thoracic surgery performed by Dr. Aaron who relied on his medical skills and faith in God.

    ISBN 0-932766-47-1
    [1. Reagan, Ronald—Assassination attempt, 1981—Fiction. 2. Surgeons—Fiction. 3. Christian life—Fiction.] I. Title. II Series.
PZ7.T373750p 1990
[Fic]—dc20
                                         97-070390
                                            CIP
                                            AC

CHAPTER 1

The Secret Service agent took one step back into the shadows of the Hilton Hotel. Removing his dark glasses, he fixed his eyes on the milling crowd of TV cameramen, reporters, and citizens all edging closer to the red velvet restraining rope. His right hand slid under his black topcoat, gripping the butt end of an Uzi machine gun. His left hand slowly lifted a miniature radio transmitter to his lips. Through earphones a dozen other agents in the area snapped to full alert when they heard him whisper, "*Rawhide's* comin'."

The doors burst open and out strode the most powerful man in the world. Looking every bit the Western code name given him, his tall, well-built frame covered the ground with great strides toward *Stagecoach*, his armored limousine waiting to whisk him off to the White House. It was a spring day in the nation's capital, and there was optimism in the President's flashing blue eyes; a rugged determination showed in his squared jaw. The crowd surged forward to get a five-second glimpse of the newly elected, fortieth President of the United States—Ronald Reagan.

He flashed his crooked smile and the TV cameras rolled. Millions of Americans watched this man of determination stride forth. They liked him—his poise, his self-assurance, his great humor. Old-timers said he had that certain cut that once made this country great—the rugged frontiersman facing incredible odds, hitching up his britches, strapping on six-shooters, bucking up his faith, and squaring off to the challenge of seemingly insurmountable odds. This republic desperately needed that dynamic leadership. Indeed, the odds were stacked against him. He'd need every bit of courage and guts his code name *Rawhide* conjured up

"Rawhide's comin'"

to face the enemy. The superpowers were chin-to-chin rattling their atomic bombs; foreign terrorists held American hostages; our staunch ally was under mortal attack.

Against this, one of Rawhide's holsters was loaded with the mightiest fighting machine the world had ever known. Hundreds of thousands of armed soldiers stood battle-ready around the world. Giant battleships and fast missile frigates patrolled every ocean on earth. An air force of thousands of the most advanced jet fighters piloted by top guns were in the air at all times. Silent submarines cruised the depths, poised to launch nuclear-armed missiles. All these were ready to defend against any enemy any-where on the globe. All Rawhide had to do was push the button.

Yet, with all this military might to defend the nation against foreign enemies, the very foundation that glued the republic together was cracking and beginning to crumble from within. Massive racial violence was erupting. Violent crime was on the rise, and running amuck was an exploding drug addiction that was eating at the very core of the nation—its youth. Torn and twisted, the backbone of the nation—its moral fiber—stood on the brink of catastrophic collapse.

This was a battle of foundational values—the collective conscience of the people. It was spiritual warfare. Against this, all the military might of the world had no effect. It would take a stronger weapon to combat this enemy. Ronald Reagan recognized this, and with prudent wisdom he reached to his other holster for his ultimate weapon—that unshakable faith in a personal Creator-God, the very thing that girded up our forefathers and made this republic great from the beginning. Rawhide knew the way to this mighty God was not through brute strength and military might, but rather prayer on bended knee; this he did, just as his predecessor George Washington had done in those desperate days at Valley Forge. The President's prayer, as the leader and heartbeat of America, was to lead this nation back to its roots—*one nation under God*.

As Rawhide strode forward, a sinister shadow crouched in the background, poised to put a stop to this man and his dedication. Death raged in the dark eyes of John Hinckley, Jr. At twenty-five years of age, this American citizen had been a member of the Nazi Party. Founded by Hitler before World War II, this political party held as its very foundation the belief that through time and chance, evolution would produce a superior race, and only the fittest would or should survive. While at the University of Texas, Hinckley studied Hitler and the Nazi Party with "an extraordinary fixation," as his professor said. He did a detailed report on Hitler's autobiography, *Mein Kampf*, in which Hitler expanded on his political ideals taken from evolution. His objective was to conquer the world by force and then eliminate those races of people he considered "unfit," thereby producing a super race—the Aryan Nazis.

After the Nazi armies had conquered Europe, Hitler ordered millions of God-fearing people to be rounded up and brought to death camps. It was in these concentration camps that the devastation of the Jews was carried out. In one camp called "Auschwitz," the prisoners were brought before a mad doctor named Mengele. Naked, alone, and under

Death raged in the dark eyes of John Hinckley, Jr.

the glare of a searchlight, each prisoner faced Mengele. A twist of his thumb to the left, and the prisoner would be marched off to slave labor. A twist of his thumb to the right, and the prisoner would be dragged off to the gas chambers, there to be shoved in with hundreds of others to be gassed and die in piles. At night their bodies would be dragged out and then stuffed into huge ovens. Those "crematoriums" would light up the night sky for miles around, burning with the bodies of men, women, and even children, that Mengele had ordered eliminated with the twist of a thumb.

Hitler ordered the devastations—Mengele was the Devastator.

Hinckley spent hours in transfixed study of Hitler's plan and propaganda of a higher race brought about by the evolutionary foundation of survival of the fittest. And now, forty years later, Hitler's same evil spirit was again rearing its ugly head through one John Hinckley, Jr.—a Nazi.

Hinckley also had a mad fascination for a young movie star he had never met. She had played the part of a teenage prostitute in a film about a demented young man who planned to kill a high political figure and then stalked his victim relentlessly. Time after time he sat through the film, burying into his drug-filled, mesmerized mind the satanic plot—stalk and kill, stalk and kill. As his plan to get the President took form in his mind, he wrote the starlet a letter. In it he said, "I would abandon this idea of getting Reagan in a second if I could only win your heart and live out the rest of my life with you. . . . I will admit to you that the reason I'm going ahead with this attempt now is because I just cannot wait any longer to impress you."

This demon-controlled, sick man went on to close the letter, "I'm asking you to please look into your heart and at least give me the chance with this historical deed to gain your respect and love."

Five months earlier, Hinckley had been picked up by the police in Nashville carrying three illegal pistols while trying to board an airplane. The President was in town that very day. Psychiatrists working for the Secret Service would brand his type as a *stalker*. Now, hunching down, he edged his way closer to the red velvet rope that restrained the crowd from the approaching President. A Pinkerton detective momentarily noticed Hinckley's nervous, fidgety actions as he shouldered his way through the crowd.

The day before (about noon on Sunday), Hinckley had arrived at the Greyhound Bus Terminal in Washington, just five blocks from the White House. He went to the Burger King and ordered, "Gimme a Whopper, cheese, no onions, and an order of onion rings." He slammed a $5 bill on the counter and snarled at the waitress when she politely asked him if it was to go. "I said it was for here."

Grabbing his tray, he went to a dark corner and, hunched over, wolfed down his food, his dark eyes glaring at the waitress from behind his upturned collar. Later, he checked into the Central Hotel only two blocks from the White House. There he paid forty-two dollars for a room with twin beds and a TV. That Sunday night he left his hotel room and went out to the pornographic stores, filling his mind with corrupting, lewd pictures. His senses were dulled by drugs, pornography, hard rock music, and Nazi doctrine—everything God opposed.

That same Sunday evening, the President relaxed in the family quarters of the White House. He cherished these peaceful evenings, having dinner with his wife Nancy and a few close friends in front of a crackling fire. A sense of closeness, comfort, and love surrounded the first family that evening. They had kept the day by worshipping Jesus Christ. The next morning the President rose, showered, breakfasted, and at 8:45 a.m. began his heavily scheduled day. At 1:30 Secretary Donovan arrived at the White House to escort the President to the Hilton Hotel for a speech to thirty-five hundred union members. During the five-minute ride, Donovan told his fellow Irishman a joke that had them both laughing as they entered the hall. After the President addressed the crowd, he departed amid cheers of support and emerged from the hotel. It was 2:25 p.m.

A police lieutenant took special interest in Hinckley as he fidgeted near the exit door; and then slouching down, Hinckley dropped from sight among the crowd. Once again fate was on the assassin's side as the officer turned his attention to the commotion of the approaching President.

Under his trench coat, Hinckley carried a .22-caliber Röhm, snub-nosed revolver. In it were six specially made bullets loaded and ready to kill. At a range of less than twenty feet, he couldn't miss. A kill-or-be-killed determination came over his eyes as he shouldered the last reporters out of his way, clearing a direct line to his fast-approaching target.

Because of the warm day, the President had not put on his bulletproof vest under his shirt. He didn't like the thing anyway—it was clumsy and restricted his chest movements. He was a man who liked to extend his arms in broad gestures, reaching to his public, embracing them to himself as if to bring his citizens—his friends—close to his heart. A reporter yelled, "Mr. President, Mr. President . . ." Smiling, while taking long strides, he raised his long left arm in a grand wave, his blue Irish eyes flashing to the left in response.

Seeing his chance, the stalker made his move. Dropping to a crouch as he shoved the last onlooker from his line of fire, he whipped out the six-shooter from under his coat, and with a professional, double-handed grip, took dead aim. In that instant all the raging venom he felt for those "unfit" was poured out on his target. His "stalk" was done; now for the "kill." The six-shooter exploded with fire and smoke. In two and a half seconds, six deadly slugs flew toward their mark. The assassin's eyes squinted and flinched with blind hatred at each pull of the trigger and exploding shell. The President's eyes froze in helpless shock.

At that exact instant, White House Press Secretary James Brady stepped forward directly into the line of fire. The first bullet caught him square in the forehead, smashing his brain and dropping him to the sidewalk, his face lying in a spreading pool of blood. One shot went wild, the next got patrolman Delahanty, who was ducking—he took a hollow-point slug in the back of the neck, dropping him next to Brady. Secret Service agent McCarthy leaped in front of the President as a human shield. At 6-foot-4 inches, 220 pounds, he took the next slug meant for the President. Hitting him in the lower rib cage, right side, the impact spun him around and knocked him backwards three feet. Crying in pain, clutching his side, his knees buckled and he crumbled to the pavement alongside Brady and Delahanty.

Police, Secret Service agents, and onlookers momentarily stunned by the confusion sprang into action. As the assassin was knocked to the ground, he got off one last shot. The bullet went wild, glancing off the armor plating on the doorsill of the limousine and piercing the door window. Secret Service agent Parr threw himself on top of the President as a shield, and the two of them crashed through the open door to the floor of the limo with a terrific impact. Parr, on top of the President, screamed at driver Drew Unrue, "Move out!" Slamming the gas pedal to the floor, Stagecoach blasted off with screaming tires. Glancing up, Parr saw a bullet hole in the window. Looking out the rear window through the smoke of burning rubber and spent powder, he could see agents with drawn machine guns, others struggling with

Seeing his chance, the stalker made his move.

the fighting assassin, and three bodies sprawled out on the bloody street.

As the President's motorcade roared down Connecticut Avenue, *Horsepower*, the Secret Service command post radio at the White House, crackled to life. "Shots fired," reported the agent in *Halfback*, the President's follow-up limousine. "Rawhide returning to *Crown*," he added, signaling that the President was on his way back to the White House.

"Rawhide not hurt. Repeat, Rawhide not hurt," Parr from Stagecoach (the President's limo), repeated a few seconds later.

From her window in a building across the street, Mrs. Criviski watched in horror as the President's motorcade screeched away, leaving the bodies of three men on the pavement. She grabbed her phone, dialed 911, and cried to the emergency dispatcher, "We need an ambulance at the Washington Hilton Hotel; people have been shot in the street."

Brady, lying face down, his head bleeding into a steel grating, was tended by a Secret Service agent who had laid his gun next to Brady's bloody head. Delahanty, the policeman, lay writhing, groaning in agony. Agent McCarthy lay silent.

A burly union representative had tackled Hinckley first, driving him to the pavement with a perfect clip. Then Secret Service agents and hotel guards piled on.

"There are eight or nine people tearing at the guy," yelled a TV commentator into his mike as he was knocked from his feet by the action.

Hinckley fought, kicked, bit, and clawed as they tore the gun from his iron grip and then clapped on handcuffs. Still he struggled. Pushing a knee in his back while grinding his face against the pavement, an agent pulled Hinckley's coat up over his head as a makeshift straitjacket. Cursing and gnashing his teeth, the madman was stuffed into the back of a police vehicle and hustled off to metropolitan police headquarters. Three ambulances screamed up and carried off Brady, Delahanty, and McCarthy.

Within minutes the area cleared and became eerily silent. Only a stunned Reagan aide stood staring in shock at the remnants of tragedy: blood-soaked bandages strewn on the sidewalk, blood dripping into the grating, and scattered, spent bullet shells. Tears welled in his eyes; his shoulders began to heave. "Oh! the devastation," he murmured softly. "Oh, the devastator!"

On the floor of Stagecoach, the President gingerly felt his side—he started to have trouble breathing. "I think I hurt myself when we landed on the riser," he gasped.

Agent Parr pulled the President to a sitting position. With all the gunfire he could take no chance that his charge hadn't been hit. He thrust his hands under Rawhide's coat, running them down his sides, under his arms, and over his chest—no blood. He ran his fingers through the shock of hair on the back of his head—still no wound.

"It felt like a hammer hit me," said the President. Then, coughing, bright red blood splattered out. Agent Parr recognized it as freshly oxygenated blood—blood that could only come from the lungs. The President was hit and hit bad.

He shouted to the driver, "Change course fast, Drew!" At the same time, he grabbed the car radio, "Horsepower, come in. Rawhide's been hurt! We're going to GW [George Washington University Hospital]. Notify the hospital Rawhide is en route."

CHAPTER 2

Three phones sat side by side in the emergency room at George Washington University Hospital. The middle one was all white—the Presidential phone which had a clear line directly to Horsepower at the White House and was to be used only in extreme emergencies. It rang. Nurse Wendy studied the phone in momentary shock. Gingerly, she picked it up. A tense, husky voice declared, "The Presidential motorcade is on its way. Prepare for immediate emergency care."

The emergency room exploded with personnel running for blood, clearing emergency tables, and alerting the trauma team.

Six floors above, Dr. Ben Aaron was just entering his office. Carrying a hot cup of coffee, he swung the door shut behind him with his foot, then walked over to his desk. He took a sip, placing the cup carefully on a coaster, and then slumped into his high-backed chair, stretching his legs out and tilting his head back toward the ceiling. Leaning forward, he switched on his desk-top radio, twisting the dial to an FM, classical music station. The music of Beethoven filled the room. Slowly he pulled off his glasses, dropping them to the desk. Leaning forward on his elbow, he gently massaged his forehead, closing his burning eyes.

"Slow down, Ben. Ease off. We've come through the storm clouds and made a landing—we're on the ground. Cool those jets." Pilot talk came easy to Dr. Aaron. Along the way to becoming a heart surgeon, he had earned his wings as an instrument-rated pilot and flight instructor. But for now, on that warm, rainy Monday afternoon, he was just one totally exhausted mortal.

Slowly he pulled off his glasses,
dropping them to the desk.

ဆ   ဆ   ဆ

Ten days prior, Dr. Aaron had performed a routine aortic valve replacement on a patient's heart. At first, all went favorably with the patient responding surprisingly well; but then over the weekend, the patient's hands began to turn blue and cold. The nurses became more alarmed when his pulse grew weak. And when they picked up an irregular heartbeat, a call went out to Dr. Aaron at home. Rushing to the hospital that Sunday, Dr. Aaron found that the patient's blood pressure had dropped, and he was disoriented.

Dr. Aaron made the decision. "Call the surgical team immediately. We're going back into his heart."

The nurses scrambled to the phones. Others began to prepare the heart room. By 10:30 that night, two anesthesiologists, a scrub nurse, a circulating nurse, two resident physicians, and Dr. Aaron were in the heart room hovering over the patient under the glare of powerful surgical lights. After the patient was anesthetized, Dr. Aaron made an incision along the old wound, cutting from the top of his breastbone to the bottom and removing the previously inserted stitches. Then, with special cutters, he snipped the wires he had installed during the first operation to hold the breastbone together, gradually opening the chest cavity.

The problem literally leaped up at the surgical team as they viewed the heart sac bulging with blood. It looked like a waterfilled balloon ready to burst. The heart was crying for help—under all that pressure, it's no wonder it had trouble beating and pumping.

The heart sac was punctured and the released blood quickly suctioned from the chest cavity. Still, fresh blood continued to flow. A look of consternation crossed the eyes of the surgical team.

"It's difficult to keep up with the flow—the guy was pumped so full of anticoagulants to thin out his blood that now it just won't clot," said the assisting surgeon operating the suction device.

"I think we'd best use the electrocoagulator," said Dr. Aaron tersely. A nurse smartly slapped the pencil-sized instrument into his hand.

Dr. Aaron's eyes flashed to the surgical assistant. "Are we grounded?"

"Patient's grounded, Doctor."

"How about you, Ben? Got your rubber shoes on?" called the assisting physician.

"You bet. I've been zapped enough to teach even this old dog. Let's fire up."

A white arc shot out of the instrument. Dr. Aaron moved it quickly over the pockets of blood, literally frying the surface blood and creating instant coagulation. Moving delicately around the heart, lung, and esophagus, he worked the device with extreme caution.

"One more spot to zap here and that should do it—there we go." Leaning back, Dr. Aaron handed his "fire stick" to the surgical nurse.

By now the patient's heart had been exposed for several hours. The tension and exhaustion were becoming evident in the eyes of the surgical team as they continued their delicate work well into the early morning hours. Indeed, anytime open-heart surgery is performed there is an element of instant life or death. No matter how experienced the surgeon, the razor's edge of life or death by a fraction, by a millisecond, haunts the recesses of the mind.

"There, we've done about all we can do—the rest is up to the Lord," said an exhausted Dr. Aaron.

"Looks like the Lord is doin' just fine where you left off, Ben," said an assistant surgeon, smiling under his mask as they all watched the patient's heart begin a robust, rhythmical beat.

As the sun rose Monday morning, Dr. Aaron went to check on his patient in the heart recovery room. All vital signs were excellent. Then turning, he walked down the hall past the scrub area, past the open-heart surgery room, and on to the locker room. He stripped his blood-stained "greens," tossing them over his shoulder into the laundry hamper. "Two for our team!" he said, gasping as ice-cold water blasted him from the huge shower nozzles. Toweling off, he slipped into fresh "greens," and then retraced his steps to the scrub area outside the heart operating room.

"I'll help you on with your mask," said the new on-duty surgical nurse. "The patient is fully prepped. You look fresh and ready this morning—probably had ten hours' sleep, right, Doctor?" she said with a wink.

"Something like that," said Dr. Aaron with a grin.

This was the heart surgeon's first scheduled, open-heart bypass case of the upcoming week. It wasn't the first time he had kicked off his fully scheduled week having spent the weekend at the hospital, grabbing what precious sleep he could get on his office couch. Holding his gloved hands up, he nodded his head toward the operating room door. "Come on, let's go get 'em, Miss Nightingale!" he said as they stepped into the amphitheater where they were greeted by a fresh surgical team.

Standing over his patient, Dr. Aaron bowed his head and asked the Lord's blessing on his hands. "May they do Your work, Lord." Then he concentrated on the procedure for a quadruple bypass open-heart operation.

Taking a scalpel, he made the incision from the top of the breastbone to the bottom, working the bottom area a bit more open. Having done that, he slipped the foot of his saber saw under the sternum and squeezed the activator button, sending the blade into an up-and-down blur. Pushing the instrument forward, he proceeded to saw the sternum in two, a slight whiff of smoke rising as the blade easily buzzed through the bone structure. Removing the saw, he inserted the chest spreader, screwing it open. With each twist, the chest cavity yawned wider, exposing the diseased heart in its protective sac, the pericardium. Carefully he cut the sac open—the heart with its four plugged arteries now in full view.

"Okay, let's get the heart-lung machine ready."

"The machine is fired up and the connecting tubes are ready, Doctor," said the assisting surgeon, placing the two, finger-sized tubes that extended from the machine onto the scrub table next to Dr. Aaron.

Before the heart could be operated on, it had to be shut down; the heart-lung machine would take over the function of the heart and the lungs by both pumping the blood and recharging it with fresh oxygen. To connect the tubes leading to the heart-lung machine, Dr. Aaron first made an incision in the aorta, the big main artery at the top of the heart where blood comes out and flows to the whole body. Into the small incision, he sutured the small tube leading back to the heart-lung machine. Once completed, he made a second incision in the right atrium, the chamber of the heart that pumps the blood to the big aorta. Into the second incision he sutured the other tube, about the size of a thumb. As the tubes cut off the blood supply to the heart and bypassed it to the heart-lung machine, the patient's heart, having no blood to pump, naturally stopped pumping; however, it continued to beat.

"Sorta looks like a flopping, deflated volleyball," said the anesthesiologist as he adjusted the anesthetic gas that kept the patient unconscious.

In order to do the delicate graft work on the heart, it would be necessary to stop the beat by cooling the heart down. The normal cooling process was accomplished by chilling the blood as it passed through the heart-lung machine. Occasionally, the heart had to be packed in ice to stop its action. What was needed for the actual grafting was an SCD heart—stopped, cold, and deflated.

By now it had been several hours into the procedure. As Dr. Aaron waited for the heart to cool, he stepped back, put his hand to his chin, and gazed at the exposed organs of his patient, pondering the magnificence of the human body. He thought of the 100 trillion tiny cells that make up the human body and the DNA segments in each cell—twenty-three segments from each parent. At conception, this DNA tape already contains the coded information that determines skin color, hair color, eye color, height, much of personality, and how every cell in the body is to function. If the DNA segments of just one cell were uncoiled, connected, and stretched out, it would be about seven feet long and so thin that details could not be seen, even under an electron microscope. And if all the DNA in the adult body were placed end-to-end, it would stretch to the moon and back over 250,000 times! If all the coded information were typed out, it would fill the Grand Canyon fifty times!

Yet, evolutionists say man came about and developed through time and chance. *That's rubbish*, he thought. Mathematically, there just wasn't enough time in billions of years to have even one tiny cell come together by chance, to say nothing about the other 99 trillion cells in a human body! Indeed, man was made with specific design by a personal Creator God!

Stepping back into the glare of the high-intensity operating lights, Dr. Aaron found himself saying Psalm 139:14 out loud, "We are *indeed* 'fearfully and wonderfully made.'"

"Amen," said the heart-lung machine operator, giving Dr. Aaron a thumbs-up to indicate the heart-lung machine was now performing all its functions for the patient.

Now that Dr. Aaron had an SCD heart, the bypass procedure could begin. The tension mounted and filled the room. Eyes darted first to the patient's leg as veins were removed, and then back to Dr. Aaron who cut them into appropriate segments to do the four bypass grafts. With incredibly delicate movements, magnified by special lenses attached to his head, Dr. Aaron sewed on the veins, bypassing the plugged areas. The tiny pieces of human tissue were no bigger around than a number two pencil lead. Not daring to even blink, with steady hands he made the tiny knots that would hold the grafts in place.

"There we are," he said to a tense team after the third bypass graft. "Just like puttin' a garden hose around a plugged sewer pipe!"

Tense eyes relaxed as masked smiles and muffled laughs broke out. The world-class surgeon had broken the incredible anxiety, putting all at ease. "Now, just one little guy to go and I think we're home free." Pushing back fatigue built up over the past thirty hours, Dr. Aaron took a deep breath. He had passed the point of exhaustion, but he reached down inside—deep down—and pulled out that extra burst of energy to persevere—runners call it going to the wall and beyond. In Dr. Aaron's case, he went to the wall and then to his Lord.

Finishing his last tiny graft, Dr. Aaron gave the order to warm the blood. Standing back, the entire surgical team fixed their eyes on the patient's heart refilling with the life-giving, warmed blood. It was that moment when all that could be done had been done—those interminable seconds when the tubes to the heart-lung machine were clamped shut. Now the heart, while filling, must start to beat and pump on its own. Would those tiny grafts perform, leak, or burst under the pressure?

"Dear Lord, if it be in Your will, breathe life back into this heart." Would that prayer he had prayed hundreds of times be answered? It took faith, "heart faith," as Dr. Aaron called it. One beat—two—then a steady, rhythmic pattern. Once more, Dr. Ben Aaron's Lord had answered his plea!

Thirty-three hours of high-tension duty with precious little sleep would drag a good doctor to the limits of human endurance, but as his fellow surgeons said, "Dr. Aaron isn't a good surgeon—he's a great surgeon." Those who knew his family from Missouri said he came from sturdy stock. His Jewish forebears emigrated from southern Russia at the turn of the century. They had fought their way to the United States, the land of their dreams, the land of freedom—freedom to carve out a decent living, freedom to worship their God, Jehovah. His hard-driving dad worked the

Texas oil fields as a roustabout on oil rigs in the boom-and-bust days of wildcat drilling and gushers. Young Ben worked his way through twelve years of medical school, internship, and special chest and heart surgery. He jogged and exercised his body into rock-hard physical shape while honing his mind razor-sharp for the rigors of becoming an open-heart surgeon. During those years he met Pat, beautiful and full of life. They married and raised four daughters. Together they attended Sunday school, together they learned the Biblical truth of Creation—that God had created all things in six, twenty-four hour days, not more than ten thousand years ago. Together they accepted Jesus Christ as their personal Savior and made Him Lord of their lives and collective family. And now, at age forty-seven, at the very pinnacle of his career, he was named the director of cardio-thoracic surgery at one of the greatest hospitals in the world—George Washington University, just a few miles from the White House—only twelve blocks from where one of the greatest dramas of the decade was unfolding before the nation and about to explode on his own world.

ფ　ფ　ფ

"We interrupt this program to announce that an attempt has been made on President Ronald Reagan's life. Moments ago at the Hilton Hotel in Washington a gunman fired shots. It is believed that the President and several others have been hit. We'll return when further information becomes available." Beethoven's music returned.

Dr. Aaron sat bolt upright at his desk. Numbed with fatigue and stunned by the news, thoughts scrambled through his mind. *Could this be real? Can this actually be happening?* Then from out the window, sixty feet below on Pennsylvania Avenue, came sounds—sounds of reality—of sirens, of screaming people, of screaming tires. For a moment he was frozen, transfixed by the horrible memory of John Kennedy's assassination—was it happening all over again?

As the Presidential motorcade careened into the emergency entrance at GW, the shrieking sound of spinning hot tires echoed down the parking ramp to a waiting paramedic who tore open the door to Stagecoach. Agent Parr leaped out, turned, and offered his hand to Rawhide. The President shrugged off the proffered help and with all the strength he could muster, stood up. He collected himself and stepped confidently for the fifteen paces to the emergency room. Every eye in the hushed crowd of agents, nurses, and emergency doctors watched as he walked with determination. Then, just clear of the walkway upon entering the ER, the President staggered.

"Catch him quick!" yelled Parr, as agents grabbed him from both sides.

His eyes rolled upward and his knees started to buckle. He turned deathly pale. A paramedic grabbed his feet while agents hoisted Rawhide by his arms and carried him into the code room—a 10-by-20-foot area where the worst emergency cases were handled.

"Let's get some oxygen on him," yelled a trauma team doctor as he rushed up, "and send out a call for Ben Aaron, fast!"

"Dr. Aaron to the emergency room. STAT!" Again the paging nurse called over the hospital intercom, this time with obvious anxiety in her voice, "Dr. Aaron to the emergency room. STAT!"

The call came at the same time his beeper activated, shocking him like a cold, wet towel in the back of the neck. Gripping the desk with his fists, he shot off a battle prayer, "Lord God Almighty, You'll have to give me strength now—I'm at the end of my rope—this will have to be on Your power!" Then, energized by his faith, the war-horse surgeon once more raced off to do surgical battle.

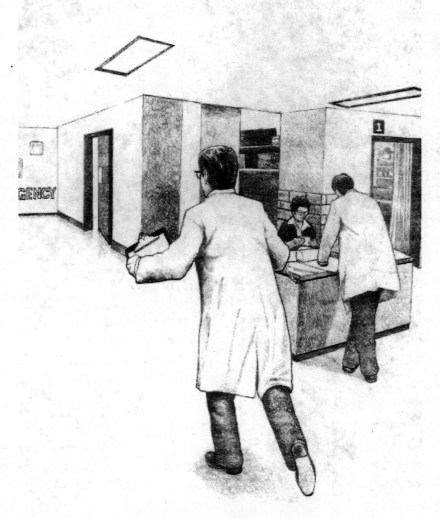

... *the war-horse surgeon once more*
raced off to do surgical battle.

CHAPTER 3

As Ben Aaron entered the ER area, a burly Secret Service agent put up his hand. "It's okay, he's Dr. Aaron, Director of Cardio-Thoracic Surgery," someone shouted. With a sideways nod from the agent, he entered the trauma bay area holding the victims.

The first person he saw was James Brady lying on his back, arms hanging limp—he looked grim, having taken a bullet in the forehead. It was hard to believe he was still alive. He then saw the President lying on a table surrounded by a bevy of nurses and trauma team doctors. A drainage tube was pouring blood out of his side, three IV tubes were in him, and he was getting oxygen. Leaning over,

Dr. Aaron examined him. Their eyes met. The President's face was pale, in stark contrast to his blue eyes. "Mr. President, I'm Dr. Aaron. I'm gonna be taking care of you. Just relax, and we'll sort this out for you."

Stepping back, he motioned to Dr. Price, who briefed him. "When they pulled up, he wanted to walk in—he was doing okay until he got to the ER. Then he collapsed and we got him on a stretcher. The nurses pulled off his jacket and cut off his shirt. I listened, but no sound from his left lung, and his blood pressure was double zero. There was no pulse. Then we got IVs and blood into him. His blood pressure's back up now to eighty with a strengthening pulse. When we rolled him over, I noticed a small slit like a button-hole under his left armpit. I think it's a bullet hole. We've got X rays on the way."

A panting orderly ran up with the just-developed X ray and Dr. Aaron held it up to the light. There it was—a bullet flattened out to the size of a dime standing on edge in the left chest area. But what's that location? Could it be? Moving to better light and adjusting his glasses, Dr. Aaron studied the X

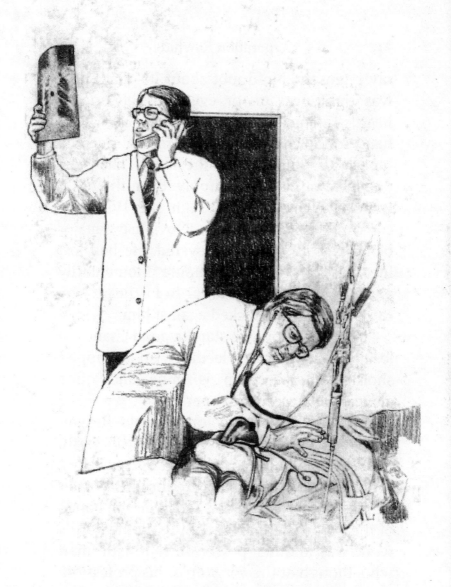

Dr. Aaron studied the X ray intensely.

ray intensely. No doubt about it—that bullet was right next to, or even possibly in the heart! Taking a step back and putting his hand to his chin, he made a mental damage report. By now the President had lost one-third of his blood supply. Even though it was being replaced through the IVs, they couldn't easily keep up. Obviously, major blood vessels had been severed. He had lost his pulse and blood pressure momentarily and had a bullet next to, or in his heart. The cards were really stacked against him.

"In my opinion, we stand a good chance of losing him if the bleeding isn't stopped shortly. The decision is mine and mine alone—we are going to operate."

Forty-five minutes before, Ronald Reagan had been the most powerful man on earth. Now, with a bullet in his chest and bleeding profusely, he had been reduced to utter helplessness. His fate was totally in the hands of the Lord. The man chosen to do the Lord's work was another powerful, self-made man who, though at the very top of his profession, was now at the bitter end of physical endurance. Both men had absolute faith in their

God; both men would have to stake everything on their Lord's promise, "My strength is made perfect in weakness" (2 Corinthians 12:9).

Leaning over the President, Dr. Aaron looked him full in the face, their eyes fixed on each other. "Mr. President, you've got a bullet in your chest. I think it's best we take you to the operating room, open your chest, get that bullet outta there, and fix up the damage."

The President's eyes cleared, and then grimacing in obvious pain, he said, "Whatever you think you need to do, I put myself in your hands. I guess we'd better get on with it." Dr. Aaron knew they had enjoined the battle.

Adding to the tension of the moment were Secret Service agents peering over Dr. Aaron's shoulder, watching his every move, listening to every word. The emergency room was full of them, weapons hardly concealed. In an assassination attempt like this, there could be other accomplices. Perhaps the initial shots were only to create pandemonium, and then in the middle of chaos, an easy kill could be made. All were suspect, including the doctor.

The agents weren't about to let anyone anywhere get another crack at Rawhide. At the news that there would be a move to the operating room, an orderly led a half-dozen agents down the hall to get outfitted with gowns and masks for preparation to be at their leader's side right through the actual operation.

The move to the operating room began, and halfway down the corridor, the President's wife Nancy came running up. Clutching her husband's hand, she gave him a walking hug, kiss, and "I love you."

With a forced smile and a wink, the President said, "Honey, I forgot to duck!"

She squeezed his hand, putting on her best brave face. Dr. Aaron beckoned for her to step aside. Taking her elbow, they moved apart from the entourage. Looking up at the doctor, her eyes clung to his—she searched every word. "He has a bullet near his heart, and it's imperative we stop the bleeding. I feel we should open up, get the bullet out, and fix the damage."

Looking down, she shuddered ever so slightly. Then looking back up, tears welled in her eyes. Grasping his hands in hers, she replied, "You're his . . . our doctor. You have our full assurance and prayers." These compassionate, well-chosen words gave Dr. Aaron a boost of encouragement and instant respect for Nancy Reagan.

As they wheeled the President's stretcher into the operating room, his wife hesitantly let her husband's hand slide from hers. Their eyes held each other until the doors slowly swung shut. She brought her trembling hands to her mouth, still staring at the closed door. Tears streamed down her cheeks. Then slowly she turned, and leaving her husband, she went to comfort the families of the other wounded men. Later, quietly and alone, she went to the hospital chapel to pray.

After scrubbing up, Dr. Aaron entered the operating room. High-intensity lights flooded the table on which the President lay face-up. Surrounding him was the scrub team lining up instruments in neat rows on towel-covered trays, ready to smartly slap them in the doctor's hand as he called for them. Behind them was a maze of computers, heart-lung machinery, and anesthetic equipment. Back in the shadows, Secret Service agents lined the walls, dutifully standing guard. Outside, filling the corridors, were TV crews and the international press, grabbing anyone and everyone for the smallest bit of information that would be instantly transmitted to the entire world. By now, the hot line between Washington and the Kremlin was abuzz, and all major world leaders were aware of the attack and waited anxiously for news. The eyes of the world were focused on that room. Into this arena came Dr. Ben Aaron, keenly aware that history was in the making; and by and large, he would do the making.

"Lord, I know You are a sovereign God who controls all events, and it's to You I commit this operation. If it be in Your will, O Lord, guide me and heal this man through these hands."

The room hushed, and all eyes focused on Dr. Aaron and the President. Reaching down, the doctor touched the President's shoulder reassuringly and explained that the anesthesiologist was going to give him a shot to put him to sleep. Tension filled the very air. Looking up, and with a distinct twinkle in his

*"O Lord, guide me and heal this man
through these hands."*

eye, the fortieth President of the United States said in a loud and clear voice, "I hope you guys are all Republicans!" A collective mask-muffled laugh broke out from doctors, nurses, and the shadowy figures along the walls. He had broken the tension and put all at ease.

Dr. Giordano, a firm Democrat, shouted from the back, "Today, we're all Republicans, Mr. President." Rawhide smiled and went under the anesthetic.

The first course of business was to make a six-inch incision between his fifth and sixth ribs, just under his breast. Having done that, Dr. Aaron inserted the rib spreader—a device that when screwed open, makes a six-inch space between the ribs so the chest cavity is visible. Normally this area is filled with the lung, but in this case, the lower lobe of the lung had collapsed like a spongy balloon losing air. The cavity was filled with an immense amount of blood. As the blood was being suctioned out, the President's heart came into view, pulsing strongly and in extraordinarily good shape.

Dr. Aaron realized he was probably the first person to ever look at a live, beating heart of a President of the United States; and just as the President is central to life in our nation, so is the heart central to the life of the human body. The heart is a perfectly organized mechanism that begins its work shortly after conception in the mother's womb. Beating, beating, three thousand times an hour, eighty thousand times a day whether at work or asleep—never resting, never stopping, millions and billions of times over a lifetime. That masterful combination of muscles and electrical impulses draws in oxygenated blood from the lungs and superboosts it to the other body organs—to the millions of receptacles on the back of the eyes that help give us sight, to the millions of nerve endings on our fingers giving us touch, to the millions of electrical connectors in the brain giving us the ability for thought, wisdom, and feelings. Feelings that are inherent to all mankind—the sensation of beauty that one feels while viewing a golden sunset across a fall-colored, hushed lake; feelings of power watching a surging, crashing ocean; feelings of love when a mother holds her newborn baby. None of these sensations—beauty, power, or love—could have just happened by time and chance. This incredibly complicated, perfectly organized, functioning, living heart could not have come about or developed by mutation over billions of years of mistakes through evolution. The most evident, perfect example of a sovereign Creator God is life itself, for only a Supreme Being has the capability of producing it—only God could have put the breath of life into this President's heart.

Now the area had been cleared of blood, and work could begin. The objective was two-fold—the bullet and the bleeder—that is, the severed vessel that was aggressively oozing out blood had to be sewn shut. The trail of the bullet started with the buttonhole-sized slit under his arm. Then the slug traversed down to his rib, hit it, and then glanced upward through the lung wall. Coursing through the lower lobe of the lung, it lodged close to, or in the heart. The bullet was not in view, but close inspection of the lung showed the heart had not been penetrated. The damaged lung tissue had led

Dr. Aaron to believe it had lodged right along the inner wall of the lung. That would put it less than a half-inch from the beating heart. The most expedient way to find it and extract it was to simply probe the area with his fingers. Lung tissue is like spongy Jell-O and quite easily separated. His first delicate moves were to no avail. Adjusting the light strapped to his head and screwing open the rib spreader a bit farther, ever so gently he probed his fingers into the damaged lung again. Still no bullet—the bleeder continued pumping, turning his white latex gloves bright red. Wait! Was that it? No, just a piece of bruised tissue. By now, the assorted gallery was getting edgy.

"The Secret Service guys and press want to know how it's going," whispered the surgical nurse.

"Tell 'em it's under control." Dr. Aaron had made the decision not to divulge any information one way or another until he had definitely cleared the problem. Only he and the Lord would know for sure. There was no sense raising or dashing hopes at this juncture—the tension was heavy enough.

"I'd better have another X ray to make sure this thing hasn't moved." Dr. Aaron held up his hands and stepped back as the X ray team moved in. Moments later, glancing at the picture, "It's still there, hasn't moved a bit. The inner lung wall is intact, so it's gotta be smack-dab against it, right there next to the heart. Well, let's have another go at it—all systems okay on the machines?"

"Blood oxygen, breathing, pulse, pressure, all okay."

Delicately, his fingers went in again. Dr. Aaron knew that one slight wrong move and the bullet just might dislodge. There are huge blood vessels that draw freshly oxygenated blood from the lungs directly into the heart and then on to the rest of the body. One tiny nudge and *whoosh!* It could embolize—that is, be sucked right into the heart and cause instant heart failure. Or it could be pumped right on through the heart to any number of other organs, like the brain, causing instant death.

Withdrawing his fingers one more time, Dr. Aaron's eyes caught sight of something on the tray table next to him—a piece of

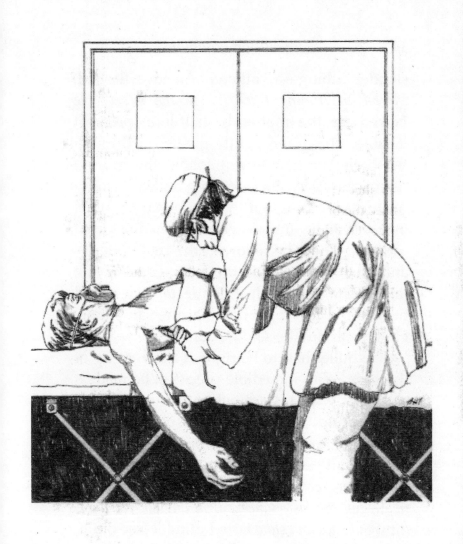

"I'll let the tubing track me to the bullet."

slender tubing—a catheter. An idea flashed. *I'll let the tubing track me to the bullet!* He picked up the foot-and-a-half-long piece of flexible tubing and gently pushed it through the bullet hole, letting it follow the bruised tissue caused by the careening bullet. Holding his breath, daring not to even blink, half-inch by half-inch, he slowly maneuvered the catheter. The tube followed the trail perfectly and then stopped at the very edge of the inner lung wall with a gentle tap. He could hear it and feel it hit home at the same time. Hissing air out, he said, "That's it!"

The bullet had to be right at the very tip of the tube. With incredible precision he made a small slit with his scalpel and then with his other hand, parted the tissue. There it was—dull gray, flattened out, standing on edge. Gently, gently, he put his thumb and forefinger over the deadly object. *Easy now—not too fast, squeeze firm but not too hard, lift it out nice and slow now.* Lifting it free of the chest cavity, he hoisted his arm up and out into the full glare of the operating lights and declared, "There it is. Thank God." A collective gasp of relief from a dozen masked faces echoed Dr. Aaron's thanks. A Secret Service agent, smiling under his mask, moved over to Dr. Aaron and motioned for him to drop the bullet in the cup he was holding out.

Dr. Aaron turned his attention to the severed, bleeding vessel that was now plainly in sight. A few sutures immediately stopped the bleeder. Now, after two hours of operating on the razor's edge, Dr. Aaron allowed himself the luxury of thanking God for once more answering his prayer—the prayer of heart faith.

That evening the President regained consciousness in the recovery room. Dr. Aaron presented him with the news that while he still had some "rough sleddin'" for a couple of days, he was indeed over the crisis and could expect a full recovery. The President was ecstatic. After giving thanks to Dr. Aaron, he gave thanks to his Lord. Later, to the assorted nurses, doctors, and visitors, he displayed that classic American wit and humor that had endeared him to many Americans:

To a nurse: "If I'd 'a gotten this much attention in Hollywood, I'd 'a never left."

To his daughter: "Looks like I ruined one of my best suits."

To his three highest White House aides: "Well, I guess I really screwed up the schedule today."

"There it is. Thank God."

CHAPTER 4

Not all the news for the President was upbeat. When informed that others had been hit and severely wounded in the hailstorm of bullets, the President bowed his head in prayer for them. Tears came to his eyes when he heard the devastating news that Press Secretary Brady, while still alive, had taken a bullet in the brain; and after five hours of surgery, it was still touch and go, minute by minute, for life or death.

The FBI brought additional sobering news, electrifying both the President and Dr. Aaron. They had run a ballistics test on the bullets used by the assassin. The bullets turned out to be a very special design for hunters to use in hunting large game. The bullet that pierced the President's chest and rested next to his heart had a hollow point, which allowed it to flatten out and cause maximum damage as it tore through flesh and bone. In addition, the slug itself had a capsule in the tip which was loaded with a chemical called lead azide. This chemically-loaded capsule was designed to detonate upon secondary impact; that is, once the bullet had entered the body and then impacted something firm, the capsule would explode, causing devastation to a six-inch area. Also, the chemical lead azide itself is highly toxic; in fact, a poison that by itself could kill.

The agents told of discovering this startling revelation while one of their ballistics experts was examining a duplicate bullet under a microscope just that day. The lead azide capsule exploded in his hands, blasting the microscope to pieces and flinging pieces of shrapnel against the agent's face. Fortunately, he was wearing plastic safety goggles and suffered only minor injury; otherwise, he would have lost his sight. As the tight-lipped agent was about to leave, he turned and said, "I think you'd be interested

DEVASTATOR
.22 cal. cartridge

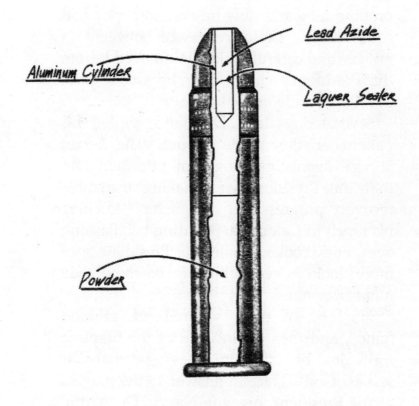

Lead Azide

Aluminum Cylinder

Laquer Sealer

Powder

"I think you'd be interested to know the name of the bullet Hinckley used."

to know the name of the bullet Hinckley used—it's called *The Devastator*."

Dr. Aaron shuddered when he thought of tapping that miniature bomb with his probing tube and how he ever so gently had squeezed the explosive device between his fingers, and carefully, slowly removed it from the President's chest. Only by God's grace did that capsule not detonate.

Several days later Dr. Aaron visited his patient at the White House. The Secret Service agents greeting him informed him that the President was making incredible recovery progress and was "itchin'" to enjoy his ranch in California. Standing tall, flashing eyes, and crooked smile, the President once more looked every bit his cowboy code name, Rawhide.

The two of them squared off, gripped hands, and then sat in front of the fireplace for a time of reflection. They agreed that it was by God's grace in answer to the prayers of the President, his wife Nancy, Dr. Aaron, and millions of American citizens that the President still had the breath of life in him, and the nation had been spared another

assassination of its President. Now that he
had been healed by God's almighty hand, it
was Ronald Reagan's prayer that the Lord
would heal the mind and heart of the young
American that had come so close to assassi-
nating him. The President of the United
States had forgiven his enemy and was
praying for him, just as his God had done for
all mankind while hanging on a cross.

President Ronald Reagan, Dr. Ben
Aaron—two powerful men brought together
for a few fleeting days in the history of this
great nation—once again firmly gripped hands,
this time in farewell. Neither man spoke, yet
their eyes affirmed to each other that deep
down—down in their hearts—they knew that
during those harrowing days their sovereign
God had absolute control of all events, and
through them had begun the process to unite
the American people and bring these United
States back to their roots—*one nation under God.*

EPILOGUE

Ronald Wilson Reagan was born February 6, 1911, in Tampico, Illinois. He was educated in Illinois public schools and was graduated from Eureka College (Illinois) in 1932 with a degree in economics and sociology.

Following a brief career as a sports broadcaster and editor, President Reagan moved to California to work in motion pictures. His film career, interrupted by three years of service in the Army Air Corps during World War II, encompassed fifty-three, feature-length motion pictures. He served six terms as president of the Screen Actors Guild and two terms as president of the Motion Picture Industry Council.

In 1966 Ronald Reagan began his public service career with his election as governor of California, serving two terms.

Ronald Reagan announced his candidacy for the GOP Presidential nomination in November 1979 and was unanimously nominated on the first ballot at the Republican National Convention in July 1980. On November 4, 1980, Ronald Reagan was elected to the Presidency with an electoral vote margin of 489-49. He was sworn in as the fortieth President of the United States on January 20, 1981.

In August 1984, the Republican Party, once again, unanimously selected Ronald Reagan as its Presidential candidate. On November 6, 1984, he won reelection, carrying forty-nine states, and was sworn in for a second term at the fiftieth presidential inaugural on January 20, 1985.

President Reagan has received a number of awards, including the National Humanitarian Award from the National Conference of Christians and Jews, City of Hope "Torch of Life" Award for Humanitarian Service, Horatio Alger Award, American Newspaper Guild

Award, Freedoms Foundation Awards, Distinguished American Award from the National Football Foundation Hall of Fame, American Patriots Hall of Fame, and Medal of Valor of the State of Israel. President Reagan was installed by Her Majesty Queen Elizabeth II as an Honorary Knight Grand Cross of the Order of Bath, and is one of twelve foreign associate members of the Academy of Moral and Political Sciences of the Institute of France.

President Reagan and his wife Nancy currently reside in Los Angeles, California. The former President continues to enjoy horseback riding and other vigorous activities at their ranch. Presently, he is working on his memoirs and speaking on issues of national interest.

ଛ   ଛ   ଛ

Dr. Ben Aaron was born in Jefferson, Missouri, and grew up in Kansas City. He received his B.A. degree from the University of Missouri in 1954 and his M.D. degree from the University of Texas in 1958. He then joined the United States Navy for what was to become a thirty-eight-year tour of duty. While in the Navy, he performed his internship, general surgery residency, and thoracic surgery residency. In 1968 he established his thoracic surgery practice at the Naval Hospital in Portsmouth, Virginia. To gain more experience in heart surgery, he took a year of fellowship at the Medical College of Virginia, and since that time, has dedicated most of his surgical efforts to operating on the heart. Following his retirement from the Navy as a captain in 1979, he accepted a position at the George Washington University Medical Center in Washington, D.C. Dr. Aaron is chief of cardio-thoracic surgery, as well as a full professor.

In 1996 he entered private practice, allowing him more time to aid in medical missions. He also serves as a valued member of the Institute for Creation Research Board of Directors.

Dr. Aaron lives in Lakeside, California, with his wife, Pat. They have been married forty-five years and have four married daughters and eight grandchildren. As well as being an instrument-rated pilot and certified flight instructor, Dr. Aaron plays golf, jogs, and enjoys scuba diving.

ABOUT THE AUTHOR

P aul Thomsen graduated from the University of Wisconsin (Madison) in 1960. Through his career as an international executive and corporate owner, he has lived in and traveled much of the world.

Paul and his wife, Julie, have created Dynamic Genesis, Inc., and endeavor to produce books for the Creation Adventure Series, of which *Operation Rawhide* is a part. They also conduct seminars for school students, teaching them how to answer questions on origins the way the public school textbooks present them, and then "qualify" their answers with a nongradable, biblical, scientific answer. This "qualifier" system has received enthusiastic approval from both teachers and students.

The Thomsens have seven children and live on a small lake in northern Wisconsin.

While in the San Diego area, visit the

Institute for Creation Research

and its *exciting*

Museum of Creation and Earth History

10946 Woodside Avenue North
Santee, California 92071
or call for information at (619) 448-0900